PILGRIMS TO THE PECOS

(Weary Pilgrims on the Road)

BY

ROBERT E. HOWARD

British Library Cataloguing-in-Publication Data
A catalogue record for this book is available from the
British Library

Robert E. Howard

Robert Ervin Howard was born in Peaster, Texas in 1906. During his youth, his family moved between a variety of Texan boomtowns, and Howard – a bookish and somewhat introverted child – was steeped in the violent myths and legends of the Old South. Although he loved reading and learning, Howard developed a distinctly Texan, hardboiled outlook on the world. He became a passionate fan of boxing, taking it up at an amateur level, and from the age of nine began to write adventure tales of semi-historical bloodshed. In 1919, when Howard was thirteen, his family moved to the Central Texas hamlet of Cross Plains, where he would stay for the rest of his life.

At fifteen Howard began to read the pulp magazines of the day, and to write more seriously. The December 1922 issue of his high school newspaper featured two of his stories, 'Golden Hope Christmas' and 'West is West'. In 1924 he sold his first piece – a short caveman tale titled 'Spear and Fang' – for $16 to the not-yet-famous *Weird Tales* magazine. He published with the magazine regularly over the next few years. 1929 was a breakout year for Howard, in that the 23-year-old writer began to sell to other magazines, such as *Ghost Stories* and *Argosy*, both of whom had previously sent him hundreds of rejection slips. In 1930, he began a correspondence with weird fiction master H. P. Lovecraft which ran up to his death six years later, and is regarded as one of the great correspondence cycles in all of fantasy literature.

It was partly due to Lovecraft's encouragement that Howard created his most famous character, Conan the Cimmerian. Conan – a barbarian-turned-King during the Hyborian Age, a mythical period of some 12,000 years ago – featured in seventeen *Weird Tales* stories between 1933 and 1936, and is now regarded as having spawned the 'sword and sorcery' genre, making Howard's influence on fantasy literature comparable to that of J. R. R. Tolkien's. The Conan stories have since been adapted many times, most famously in the series of films starring Arnold Schwarzenegger.

Howard was enjoying an all-time high in sales by the beginning of 1936, but he was also deeply upset by the ill health of his mother, who had fallen into a coma. On the morning of June 11, 1936, he asked an attending nurse whether she would ever recover, and the nurse replied negatively. Howard walked to his car, parked outside the family home in Cross Plains, and shot himself. He died eight hours later, aged just thirty.

That there wagon rolled up the trail and stopped in front of our cabin one morning jest after sun-up. We all come out to see who it was, because strangers ain't common on Bear Creek--and not very often welcome, neither. They was a long, hungry-looking old coot driving, and four or five growed boys sticking their heads out.

"Good mornin', folks," said the old coot, taking off his hat. "My name is Joshua Richardson. I'm headin' a wagon-train of immigrants which is lookin' for a place to settle. The rest of 'em's camped three miles back down the trail. Everybody we met in these here Humbolt Mountings told us we'd hev to see Mister Roaring Bill Elkins about settlin' here-abouts. Be you him?"

"I'm Bill Elkins," says pap suspiciously.

"Well, Mister Elkins," says Old Man Richardson, wagging his chin-whiskers, "we'd admire it powerful if you folks would let us people settle somewheres about."

"Hmmmm!" says pap, pulling his beard. "Whar you all from?"

"Kansas," says Old Man Richardson.

"Ouachita," says pap, "git my shotgun."

"Don't you do no sech thing, Ouachie," says maw. "Don't be stubborn, Willyum. The war's been over for years."

"That's what I say," hastily spoke up Old Man Richardson. "Let bygones be bygones, I says!"

"What," says pap ominously, "is yore honest opinion of General Sterlin' Price?"

"One of nature's noblemen!" declares Old Man Richardson earnestly.

"Hmmmmm!" says pap. "You seem to have considerable tact and hoss-sense for a Red-laig. But they hain't no more room on Bear Creek fer no more settlers, even if they was Democrats. They's nine er ten families now within a rech of a hunnert square miles, and I don't believe in over-crowdin' a country."

"But we're plumb tuckered out!" wailed Old Man Richardson. "And nowheres to go! We hev been driv from pillar to post, by settlers which got here ahead of us and grabbed all the best land. They claims it whether they got any legal rights or not."

"Legal rights be damned," snorted pap. "Shotgun rights is what goes in this country. But I know jest the place fer you. It's ten er fifteen days' travel from here, in Arizony. It's called Bowie Knife Canyon, and hit's jest right fer farmin' people, which I jedge you all be."

"We be," says Old Man Richardson. "But how we goin' to git there?"

"My son Breckinridge will be plumb delighted to guide you there," says pap. "Won't you, Breckinridge?"

"No, I won't," I said. "Why the tarnation have I got to be picked on to ride herd on a passle of tenderfooted mavericks--"

"He'll git you there safe," says pap, ignoring my remarks. "He dotes on lendin' folks a helpin' hand, don't you, Breckinridge?"

Seeing the futility of argyment, I merely snarled and went to saddle Cap'n Kidd. I noticed Old Man Richardson and his boys looking at me in a very pecooliar manner all the time, and when I come out on Cap'n Kidd, him snorting and bucking and kicking the rails out of the corral like he always does, they turnt kind of pale and Old Man Richardson said: "I wouldn't want to impose on yore son, Mister Elkins. After all, we wasn't intendin' to go to that there canyon, in the first place--"

"I'm guidin' you to Bowie Knife Canyon!" I roared. "Maybe you warn't goin' there before I saddled my hoss, but you air now! C'm'on."

I then cut loose under the mules' feet with my .45s to kind of put some ginger in the critters, and they brayed and sot off down the trail jest hitting the high places with Old Man Richardson hanging onto the lines and bouncing all over the seat and his sons rolling in the wagon-bed.

WE COME INTO CAMP full tilt, and some of the men grabbed their guns and the women hollered and jerked up their kids, and one feller was so excited he fell into a big

5

pot of beans which was simmering over a fire and squalled out that the Injuns was trying to burn him alive.

Old Man Richardson had his feet braced again the front-gate, pulling back on the lines as hard as he could and yelling bloody murder, but the mules had the bits betwixt their teeth. So I rode to their heads and grabbed 'em by the bridles and throwed 'em back onto their haunches, and Old Man Richardson ought to of knew the stop would be sudden. T'warn't my fault he done a dive off of the seat and hit on the wagon-tongue on his head. And it warn't my fault neither that one of the mules kicked him and t'other'n bit him before I could ontangle him from amongst them. Mules is mean critters howsoever you take 'em.

Everybody hollered amazing, and he riz up and mopped the blood offa his face and waved his arms and hollered: "Ca'm down, everybody! This hain't nawthin' to git excited about. This gent is Mister Breckinridge Elkins, which has kindly agreed to guide us to a land of milk and honey down in Arizony."

They received the news without enthusiasm. They was about fifty of 'em, mostly women, chillern, and half-grown young 'uns. They warn't more'n a dozen fit fighting men in the train. They all looked like they'd been on the trail a long time. And they was all some kin to Old Man Richardson--sons and daughters, and grandchillern, and nieces and nephews, and their husbands and wives, and sech like. They was one real purty gal, the old man's youngest daughter Betty, who warn't yet married.

They'd jest et breakfast and was hitched up when we arrove, so we pulled out without no more delay. I rode along of Old Man Richardson's wagon, which went ahead with the others strung out behind, and he says to me: "If this here Bowie Knife Canyon is sech a remarkable place, why ain't it already been settled?"

"Aw, they was a settlement there," I said, "but the Apaches kilt some, and Mexicans bandits kilt some, and about three years ago the survivors got to fightin' amongst theirselves and jest kind of kilt each other off."

He yanked his beard nervously and said: "I dunno! I dunno! Maybe we had ought to hunt a more peaceful spot than that there sounds like."

"You won't find no peaceful spots west of the Pecos," I assured him. "Say no more about it. I've made up our minds that Bowie Knife Canyon is the place for you all, and we're goin' there!"

"I wouldn't think of argyin' the p'int," he assured me hastily. "What towns does we pass on our way."

"Jest one," I said. "War Smoke, right on the Arizona line. Tell yore folks to keep out of it. It's a hangout for every kind of a outlaw. I jedge yore boys ain't handy enough with weppins to mix in sech company."

"We don't want no trouble," says he. "I'll tell 'em."

SO WE ROLLED ALONG, and the journey was purty uneventful except for the usual mishaps which generally happens to tenderfeet. But we progressed, until we was within striking distance of the Arizona border. And there we hit a snag. The rear wagon bogged in a creek we had to cross a few miles north of the line. They'd been a head rise, and the wagons churned the mud so the last one stuck fast. It was getting on toward sun-down, and I told the others to go on and make camp a mile west of War Smoke, and me and the folks in the wagon would foller when we got it out.

But that warn't easy. It was mired clean to the hubs, and the mules was up to their bellies. We pried and heaved and hauled, and night was coming on, and finally I said: "If I could git them cussed mules out of my way, I might accomplish somethin'."

So we unhitched 'em from the wagon, but they was stuck too, and I had to wade out beside 'em and lift 'em out of the mud one by one and tote 'em to the bank. A mule is a helpless critter. But then, with them out of the way, I laid hold of the tongue and hauled the wagon out of the creek in short order. Them Kansas people sure did look surprized, I dunno why.

Time we'd scraped the mud offa the wagon and us, and hitched up the mules again, it was night, and so it was long after dark when we come up to the camp the rest of the train had made in the place I told 'em. Old Man Richardson come up to me looking worried, and he says: "Mister Elkins, some of the boys went into that there town in spite of what I told 'em."

"Don't worry," I says. "I'll go git 'em."

I clumb on Cap'n Kidd without stopping to eat supper, and rode over to War Smoke, and tied my hoss outside the only saloon they was there. It was a small town, and awful hard looking. As I went into the saloon I seen the four Richardson boys, and they was surrounded by a gang of cut-throats and outlaws. They was a Mexican there, too, a tall, slim cuss, with a thin black mustash, and gilt braid onto his jacket.

"So you theenk you settle in Bowie Knife Canyon, eh?" he says, and one of the boys said: "Well, that's what we was aimin' to do."

"I theenk not," he said, grinning like a cougar, and I seen his hands steal to the ivory-handled guns at his hips. "You never heard of Senor Gonzeles Zamora? No? Well, he is a beeg hombre in thees country, and he has use for thees canyon in hees business."

"Start the fireworks whenever yo're ready, Gomez," muttered a white desperado. "We're backin' yore play."

The Richardson boys didn't know what the deal was about, but they seen they was up agen real trouble, and they turnt pale and looked around like trapped critters, seeing nothing but hostile faces and hands gripping guns.

"Who tell you you could settle thees canyon?" ast Gomez. "Who breeng you here? Somebody from Kansas? Yes? No?"

"No," I said, shouldering my way through the crowd. "My folks come from Texas. My granddaddy was at San Jacinto. You remember that?"

His hands fell away from his guns and his brown hide turnt ashy. The rest of them renegades give back, muttering: "Look out, boys! It's Breckinridge Elkins!"

They all suddenly found they had business at the bar, or playing cards, or something, and Gomez found hisself standing alone. He licked his lips and looked sick, but he tried to keep up his bluff.

"You maybe no like what I say about Senor Zamora?" says he. "But ees truth. If I tell him gringoes come to Bowie Knife Canyon, he get very mad!"

"Well, suppose you go tell him now," I said, and so as to give him a good start, I picked him up and throwed him through the nearest winder.

He picked hisself up and staggered away, streaming blood and Mex profanity, and them in the saloon maintained a kind of pallid silence. I hitched my guns forard, and said to the escaped convict which was tending bar, I says: "You don't want me to pay for that winder, do you?"

"Oh, no!" says he, polishing away with his rag at a spittoon he must of thought was a beer mug. "Oh, no, no, no! We needed that winder busted fer the ventilation!"

"Then everybody's satisfied," I suggested, and all the hoss-thieves and stagecoach bandits in the saloon give me a hearty agreement.

"That's fine," I says. "Peace is what I aim to have, if I have to lick every--in the joint to git it. You boys git back to the camp."

They was glad to do so, but I lingered at the bar, and bought a drink for a train-robber I'd knowed at Chawed Ear onst, and I said: "Jest who is this cussed Zamora that Mex was spielin' about?"

"I dunno," says he. "I never heard of him before."

"I wouldn't say you was lyin'," I said tolerantly. "Yo're jest sufferin' from loss of memory. Frequently cases like that is cured and their memory restored by a severe shock or jolt like a lick onto the head. Now then, if I was to take my six-shooter butt and drive yore head through that whiskey barrel with it, I bet it'd restore yore memory right sudden."

"Hold on!" says he in a hurry. "I jest remembered that Zamora is the boss of a gang of Mexicans which claims Bowie Knife Canyon. He deals in hosses."

"You mean he steals hosses," I says, and he says: "I ain't argyin'. Anyway, the canyon is very convenient for his business, and if you dump them immigrants in his front yard, he'll be very much put out."

"He sure will," I agreed. "As quick as I can git my hands onto him."

I finished my drink and strode to the door and turnt suddenly with a gun in each hand. The nine or ten fellers which had drawed their guns aiming to shoot me in the back as I went through the door, they dropped their weppins and throwed up their hands and yelled: "Don't shoot!" So I jest shot the lights out, and then went out and got onto Cap'n Kidd whilst them idjits was hollering and falling over each other in the dark, and rode out of War Smoke, casually shattering a few winder lights along the street as I went.

When I got back to camp the boys had already got there, and the whole wagon train was holding their weppins and scairt most to death.

"I'm mighty relieved to see you back safe, Mister Elkins," says Old Man Richardson. "We heard the shootin' and was afeared them bullies had kilt you. Le's hitch up and pull out right now!"

Them tenderfoots is beyond my comprehension. They'd of all pulled out in the dark if I'd let 'em, and I believe most of 'em stayed awake all night, expecting to be butchered in their sleep. I didn't say nothing to them about Zamora. The boys hadn't understood what Gomez was talking about, and they warn't no use getting 'em worse scairt than what they generally was.

WELL, WE PULLED OUT before daylight, because I aimed to rech the canyon without another stop. We kept rolling and got there purty late that night. It warn't really no canyon at all, but a whopping big valley, well timbered, and mighty good water and grass. It was a perfect place for a settlement, as I p'inted out, but tenderfoots is powerful pecooliar. I happened to pick our camp site that night on the spot where the Apaches wiped out a mule-train of Mexicans six years before, and it was too dark to see the bones scattered around till next morning. Old Man Richardson was using what he thought was a round rock for a piller, and when he woke up the next morning and found he'd been sleeping with his head onto a human skull he like to throwed a fit.

And when I wanted to stop for the noonday meal in that there grove where the settlers hanged them seven cattle-rustlers three years before, them folks got the willies when they seen some of the ropes still sticking onto the limbs, and wouldn't on no account eat their dinner there. You got no idee what pecooliar folks them immigrants is till you've saw some.

Well, we stopped a few miles further on, in another grove in the midst of a wide rolling country with plenty of trees and tall grass, and I didn't tell 'em that was where them outlaws murdered the three Grissom boys in their sleep. Old

Man Richardson said it looked like as good a place as any to locate the settlement. But I told him we was going to look over the whole derned valley before we chosed a spot. He kind of wilted and said at least for God's sake let 'em rest a few days.

I never seen folks which tired out so easy, but I said all right, and we camped there that night. I hadn't saw no signs of Zamora's gang since we come into the valley, and thought likely they was all off stealing hosses somewhere. Not that it made any difference.

Early next morning Ned and Joe, the old man's boys, they wanted to look for deer, and I told 'em not to go more'n a mile from camp, and be keerful, and they said they would, and sot out to the south.

I went back of the camp a mile or so to the creek where Jim Dornley ambushed Tom Harrigan four years before, and taken me a swim. I stayed longer'n I intended to, it was sech a relief to get away from them helpless tenderfoots for a while, and when I rode back into camp, I seen Ned approaching with a stranger--a young white man, which carried hisself with a air of great importance.

"Hey, pap!" hollered young Ned as they dismounted. "Where's Mister Elkins? This feller says we can't stay in Bowie Knife Canyon!"

"Who're you?" I demanded, emerging from behind a wagon, and the stranger's eyes bugged out as he seen me.

"My name's George Warren," says he. "A wagon train of us just came into the valley from the east yesterday. We're from Illinois."

"And by what right does you order people outa this canyon?" I ast.

"We got the fightin'est man in the world guidin' us," says he. "I thought he was the biggest man in the world till I seen you. But he ain't to be fooled with. When he heard they was another train in the valley, he sent me to tell you to git. You better, too, if you got any sense!"

"We don't want no trouble!" quavered Old Man Richardson.

"You got a nerve!" I snorted, and I pulled George Warren's hat down so the brim come off and hung around his neck like a collar, and turnt him around and lifted him off the ground with a boot in the pants, and then throwed him bodily onto his hoss. "Go back and tell yore champeen that Bowie Knife Canyon belongs to us!" I roared, slinging a few bullets around his hoss' feet. "And we gives him one hour to hitch up and clear out!"

"I'll git even for this!" wept George Warren, as he streaked it for his home range. "You'll be sorry, you big polecat! Jest wait'll I tell Mister--" I couldn't catch what else he said.

"Now I bet he's mad," says Old Man Richardson. "We better go. After all--"

"Shet up!" I roared. "This here valley's our'n, and I intends to defend our rights to the last drop of yore blood! Hitch them mules and swing the wagons in a circle! Pile yore saddles and plunder betwixt the wheels. I got a idee you all fights better behind breastworks. Did you see their camp, Ned?"

"Naw," says he, "but George Warren said it lies about three miles east of our'n. Me and Joe got separated and I was swingin' east around the south end of that ridge over there, when I met this George Warren. He said he was out lookin' for a hoss before sun-up and seen our camp and went back and told their guide, and he sent him over to tell us to git out."

"I'm worried about Joe," said Old Man Richardson. "He ain't come back."

"I'll go look for him," I said. "I'll also scout their camp, and if the odds ain't more'n ten to one, we don't wait for 'em to attack. We goes over and wipes 'em out pronto. Then we hangs their fool sculps to our wagon bows as a warnin' to other sech scoundrels."

Old Man Richardson turnt pale and his knees knocked together, but I told him sternly to get to work swinging them wagons, and clumb onto Cap'n Kidd and lit out.

REASON I HADN'T SAW the smoke of the Illinois camp was on account of a thick-timbered ridge which lay east of our camp. I swung around the south end of that ridge and headed east, and I'd gone maybe a mile and a half when I seen a man riding toward me.

When he seen me he come lickety-split, and I could see the sun shining on his Winchester barrel. I cocked my .45-90 and rode toward him and we met in the middle of a open flat. And suddenly we both lowered our weppins and pulled up, breast to breast, glaring at each other.

"Breckinridge Elkins!" says he.

"Cousin Bearfield Buckner!" says I. "Air you the man which sent that unlicked cub of a George Warren to bring me a defiance?"

"Who else?" he snarled. He always had a awful temper.

"Well," I says, "this here is our valley. You all got to move on."

"What you mean, move on?" he yelled. "I brung them pore critters all the way from Dodge City, Kansas, where I encountered 'em bein' tormented by some wuthless buffalo hunters which is no longer in the land of the livin'. I've led 'em through fire, flood, hostile Injuns and white renegades. I promised to lead 'em into a land of milk and honey, and I been firm with 'em, even when they weakened theirselves. Even when they begged on bended knees to be allowed to go back to Illinois, I wouldn't hear of it, because, as I told 'em, I knowed what was best for 'em. I had this canyon in mind all the time. And now you tells me to move on!"

17

Cousin Bearfield rolled an eye and spit on his hand. I jest waited.

"What sort of a reply does you make to my request to go on and leave us in peace?" he goes on. "George Warren come back to camp wearin' his hat brim around his neck and standin' up in the stirrups because he was too sore to set in the saddle. So I set 'em fortifyin' the camp whilst I went forth to reconnoiter. That word I sent you, I now repeats in person. Yo're my blood-kin, but principles comes first!"

"Me, too," I said. "A Nevada Elkins' principles is as loftey as a Texas Buckner's any day. I whupped you a year ago in Cougar Paw--"

"That's a cussed lie!" gnashed he. "You taken a base advantage and lammed me with a oak log when I warn't expectin' it!"

"Be that as it may," says I, "--ignorin' the fack that you had jest beaned me with a rock the size of a water-bucket-- the only way to settle this dispute is to fight it out like gents. But we got to determine what weppins to use. The matter's too deep for fists."

"I'd prefer butcher knives in a dark room," says he, "only they ain't no room. If we jest had a couple of sawed-off shotguns, or good double-bitted axes--I tell you, Breck, le's tie our left hands together and work on each other with our bowies."

"Naw," I says, "I got a better idee. We'll back our hosses together, and then ride for the oppersite sides of the flat. When we git there we'll wheel and charge back, shootin' at each other with our Winchesters. Time they're empty we'll be clost enough to use our pistols, and when we've emptied them we'll be clost enough to finish the fight with our bowies."

"Good idee!" agreed Bearfield. "You always was a brainy, cultured sort of a lobo, if you wasn't so damn stubborn. Now, me, I'm reasonable. When I'm wrong, I admit it."

"You ain't never admitted it so far," says I.

"I ain't never been wrong yet!" he roared. "And I'll kyarve the gizzard of the buzzard which says I am! Come on! Le's git goin'."

So we started to gallop to the oppersite sides of the flat when I heard a voice hollering: "Mister Elkins! Mister Elkins!"

"Hold on!" I says. "That's Joe Richardson."

NEXT MINUTE JOE COME tearing out of the bresh from the south on a mustang I hadn't never seen before, with a Mexican saddle and bridle on. He didn't have no hat nor shirt, and his back was criss-crossed with bloody streaks. He likewise had a cut in his sculp which dribbled blood down his face.

"Mexicans!" he panted. "I got separated from Ned and rode further'n I should ought to had. About five miles down the canyon I run into a big gang of Mexicans--about thirty of 'em. One was that feller Gomez. Their leader was a big feller they called Zamora.

"They grabbed me and taken my hoss, and whupped me with their quirts. Zamora said they was goin' to wipe out every white man in the canyon. He said his scouts had brung him news of our camp, and another'n east of our'n, and he aimed to destroy both of 'em at one sweep. Then they all got onto their hosses and headed north, except one man which I believe they left there to kill me before he follered 'em. He hit me with his six-shooter and knocked me down, and then put up his gun and started to cut my throat with his knife. But I wasn't unconscious like he thought, and I grabbed his gun and knocked him down with it, and jumped on his hoss and lit out. As I made for camp I heard you and this gent talkin' loud to each other, and headed this way."

"Which camp was they goin' for first?" I demanded.

"I dunno," he said. "They talked mostly in Spanish I can't understand."

"The duel'll have to wait," I says. "I'm headin' for our camp."

"And me for mine," says Bearfield. "Lissen: le's decide it this way: one that scuppers the most Greasers wins and t'other'n takes his crowd and pulls out!"

"Bueno!" I says, and headed for camp.

The trees was dense. Them bandits could of passed either to the west or the east of us without us seeing 'em. I quickly left Joe, and about a quarter of a mile further on I heard a sudden burst of firing and screaming, and then silence. A little bit later I bust out of the trees into sight of the camp, and I cussed earnestly. Instead of being drawed up in a circle, with the men shooting from between the wheels and holding them bandits off like I expected, them derned wagons was strung out like they was heading back north. The hosses was cut loose from some of 'em, and mules was laying acrost the poles of the others, shot full of lead. Women was screaming and kids was squalling, and I seen young Jack Richardson laying face down in the ashes of the campfire with his head in a puddle of blood.

Old Man Richardson come limping toward me with tears running down his face. "Mexicans!" he blubbered. "They hit us like a harrycane jest a little while ago! They shot Jack down like he was a dog! Three or four of the other boys is got knife slashes or bullet marks or bruises from loaded quirt-ends! As they rode off they yelled they'd come back and kill us all!"

"Why'n't you throw them wagons round like I told you?" I roared.

"We didn't want no fightin'!" he bawled. "We decided to pull out of the valley and find some more peaceful place--"

"And now Jack's dead and yore stock's scattered!" I raged. "Jest because you didn't want to fight! What the hell you ever cross the Pecos for if you didn't aim to fight nobody? Set the boys to gatherin' sech stock as you got left--"

"But them Mexicans taken Betty!" he shrieked, tearing his scanty locks. "Most of 'em headed east, but six or seven grabbed Betty right out of the wagon and rode off south with her, drivin' the hosses they stole from us!"

"Well, git yore weppins and foller me!" I roared. "For Lord's sake forgit they is places where sheriffs and policemen pertecks you, and make up yore minds to fight! I'm goin' after Betty."

I HEADED SOUTH AS HARD as Cap'n Kidd could run. The reason I hadn't met them Mexicans as I rode back from the flat where I met Cousin Bearfield was because they swung around the north end of the ridge when they headed east. I hadn't gone far when I heard a sudden burst of firing, off to the east, and figgered they'd hit the Illinois camp. But I reckoned Bearfield had got there ahead of 'em. Still, it didn't seem like the shooting was far enough off to be at the other camp. But I didn't have no time to study it.

Them gal-thieves had a big start, but it didn't do no good. I hadn't rode over three miles till I heard the stolen hosses running ahead of me, and in a minute I bust out into a open flat and seen six Mexicans driving them critters at full speed, and one of 'em was holding Betty on the saddle in front of him. It was that blasted Gomez.

I come swooping down onto 'em, with a six-shooter in my right hand and a bowie knife in my left. Cap'n Kidd needed no guiding. He'd smelt blood and fire and he come like a hurricane on Jedgment Day, with his mane flying and his hoofs burning the grass.

The Mexicans seen I'd ride 'em down before they could get acrost the flat and they turnt to meet me, shooting as they come. But Mexicans always was rotten shots. As we come together I let bam three times with my .45, and: "Three!" says I.

One of 'em rode at me from the side and clubbed his rifle and hit at my head, but I ducked and made one swipe with my bowie. "Four!" says I. Then the others turnt and high-tailed it, letting the stolen hosses run where they wanted to. One of 'em headed south, but I was crowding Gomez so clost he whirled around and lit a shuck west.

"Keep back or I keel the girl!" he howled, lifting a knife, but I shot it out of his hand, and he give a yowl and let go of her and she fell off into the high grass. He kept fogging it.

I pulled up to see if Betty was hurt, but she warn't--jest scairt. The grass cushioned her fall. I seen her pap and sech of the boys as was able to ride was all coming at a high run, so I left her to 'em and taken in after Gomez again. Purty soon he looked back and seen me overhauling him, so he reched for his Winchester which he'd evidently jest thought of using, when about that time his hoss stepped into a prairie dog hole and throwed him over his head. Gomez never twitched after he hit the ground. I turnt around and rode back, cussing disgustedly, because a Elkins is ever truthful, and I couldn't honestly count Gomez in my record.

But I thought I'd scuttle that coyote that run south, so I headed in that direction. I hadn't gone far when I heard a lot of hosses running somewhere ahead of me and to the east, and then presently I bust out of the trees and come onto a flat which run to the mouth of a narrer gorge opening into the main canyon.

On the left wall of this gorge-mouth they was a ledge about fifty foot up, and they was a log cabin on that ledge with loop-holes in the walls. The only way up onto the ledge was a log ladder, and about twenty Mexicans was running their hosses toward it, acrost the flat. Jest as I reched the aidge of the bushes, they got to the foot of the wall and jumped off their hosses and run up that ladder like monkeys, letting their hosses run any ways. I seen a big feller with gold ornaments on his sombrero which I figgered was Zamora, but before I could unlimber my Winchester they was all in the cabin and slammed the door.

THE NEXT MINUTE COUSIN Bearfield busted out of the trees a few hundred yards east of where I was and started recklessly acrost the flat. Imejitely all them Mexicans started shooting at him, and he grudgingly retired into the bresh again, with terrible language. I yelled, and rode toward him, keeping to the trees.

"How many you got?" he bellered as soon as he seen me.

"Four," I says, and he grinned like a timber wolf and says: "I got five! I was ridin' for my camp when I heard the shootin' behind me, and so I knowed it was yore camp they hit first. I turnt around to go back and help you out--"

"When did I ever ast you for any help?" I bristled, but he said: "But purty soon I seen a gang of Mexicans comin' around the north end of the ridge, so I taken cover and shot five of 'em out of their saddles. They must of knowed it was me, because they high-tailed it."

"How could they know that, you conceited jackass?" I snorted. "They run off because they probably thought a whole gang had ambushed 'em."

Old Man Richardson and his boys had rode up whilst we was talking, and now he broke in with some heat, and said: "That hain't the question! The p'int is we got 'em hemmed up on that ledge for the time bein', and can git away before they come down and massacre us."

"What you talkin' about?" I roared. "They're the ones which is in need of gittin' away. If any massacrein' is did around here, we does it!"

"It's flyin' in the face of Providence!" he bleated, but I told him sternly to shet up, and Bearfield says: "Send somebody over to my camp to bring my warriors," so I told Ned to go and he pulled out.

Then me and Bearfield studied the situation, setting our hosses in the open whilst bullets from the cabin whistled all around us, and the Richardsons hid in the bresh and begged us to be keerful.

"That ledge is sheer on all sides," says Bearfield. "Nobody couldn't climb down onto it from the cliff. And anybody tryin' to climb that ladder in the teeth of twenty Winchesters would be plum crazy."

But I says, "Look, Bearfield, how the ledge overhangs about ten foot to the left of that ladder. A man could stand at the foot of the bluff there and them coyotes couldn't see to shoot him."

"And," says Bearfield, "he could sling his rope up over that spur of rock at the rim, and they couldn't shoot it off. Only way to git to it would be to come out of the cabin and rech down and cut it with a knife. Door opens toward the ladder, and they ain't no door in the wall on that side. A man could climb right up onto the ledge before they knowed it--if they didn't shoot him through the loop-holes as he come over the rim."

"You stay here and shoot 'em when they tries to cut the rope," I says.

"You go to hell!" he roared. "I see through yore hellish plot. You aims to git up there and kill all them Mexes before I has a chance at 'em. You thinks you'll outwit me! By golly, I got my rights, and--"

"Aw, shet up," I says disgustedly. "We'll both go." I hollered to Old Man Richardson: "You all lay low in the bresh and shoot at every Mex which comes outa the cabin."

"What you goin' to do now?" he hollered. "Don't be rash--"

But me and Bearfield was already headed for the ledge at a dead run.

THIS MOVE SURPRIZED the Mexicans, because they knowed we couldn't figger to ride our hosses up that ladder. Being surprized they shot wild and all they done was graze my sculp and nick Bearfield's ear. Then, jest as they begun to get their range and started trimming us clost, we swerved aside and thundered in under the overhanging rock.

We clumb off and tied our hosses well apart, otherwise they'd of started fighting each other. The Mexicans above us was yelling most amazing but they couldn't even see us, much less shoot us. I whirled my lariat, which is plenty longer and stronger than the average lasso, and roped the spur of rock which jutted up jest below the rim.

"I'll go up first," says I, and Bearfield showed his teeth and drawed his bowie knife.

27

"You won't neither!" says he. "We'll cut kyards! High man wins!"

So we squatted, and Old Man Richardson yelled from the trees: "For God's sake, what are you doin' now? They're fixin' to roll rocks down onto you!"

"You tend to yore own business," I advised him, and shuffled the cards which Bearfield hauled out of his britches. As it turnt out, the Mexes had a supply of boulders in the cabin. They jest opened the door and rolled 'em toward the rim. But they shot off the ledge and hit beyond us.

Bearfield cut, and yelped: "A ace! You cain't beat that!"

"I can equal it," I says, and drawed a ace of diamonds.

"I wins!" he clamored. "Hearts beats diamonds!"

"That rule don't apply here," I says. "It war a draw, and--"

"Why, you--!" says Bearfield, leaning for'ard to grab the deck, and jest then a rock about the size of a bushel basket come bounding over the ledge and hit a projection which turnt its course, so instead of shooting over us, it fell straight down and hit Bearfield smack between the ears.

It stunned him for a instant, and I jumped up and started climbing the rope, ignoring more rocks which come thundering down. I was about half-way up when Bearfield come to, and he riz with a beller of rage. "Why, you dirty, double-crossin' so-and-so!" says he, and started throwing rocks at me.

They was a awful racket, the Mexicans howling, and guns banging, and Bearfield cussing, and Old Man Richardson wailing: "They're crazy, I tell you! They're both crazy as mudhens! I think everybody west of the Pecos must be maneyacks!"

Bearfield grabbed the rope and started climbing up behind me, and about that time one of the Mexicans run to cut the rope. But for onst my idiotic follerers was on the job. He run into about seven bullets that hit him all to onst, and fell down jest above the spur where the loop was caught onto.

So when I reched my arm over the rim to pull myself up they couldn't see me on account of the body. But jest as I was pulling myself up, they let go a boulder at random and it bounded along and bounced over the dead Mexican and hit me right smack in the face. It was about as big as a pumpkin.

I give a infuriated beller and swarmed up onto the ledge and it surprized 'em so that most of them missed me clean. I only got one slug through the arm. Before they had time to shoot again I made a jump to the wall and flattened myself between the loop-holes, and grabbed the rifle barrels they poked through the loop-holes and bent 'em and rooint 'em. Bearfield was coming up the rope right behind me, so I grabbed hold of the logs and tore that whole side of the wall out, and the roof fell in and the other walls come apart.

* * *

IN A INSTANT ALL YOU could see was logs falling and rolling and Mexicans busting out into the open. Some got pinned by the falling logs and some was shot by my embattled Kansans and Bearfield's Illinois warriors which had jest come up, and some fell offa the ledge and broke their fool necks.

One of 'em run agen me and tried to stab me so I throwed him after them which had already fell off the ledge, and hollered: "Five for me, Bearfield!"

"--!" says Bearfield, arriving onto the scene with blood in his eye and his bowie in his hand. Seeing which a big Mexican made for him with a butcher knife, which was pore jedgment on his part, and in about the flick of a mustang's tail Bearfield had a sixth man to his credit.

This made me mad. I seen some of the Mexicans was climbing down the ladder, so I run after 'em, and one turnt around and missed me so close with a shotgun he burnt my eyebrows. I taken it away from him and hit him over the head with it, and yelled: "Six for me, too, Cousin Bearfield!"

"Lookout!" he yelled. "Zamora's gittin' away!"

I seen Zamora had tied a rope to the back side of the ledge and was sliding down it. He dropped the last ten feet and run for a corral which was full of hosses back up the gorge, behind the ledge.

We seen the other Mexicans was all laid out or running off up the valley, persued by our immigrants, so I went down the ladder and Bearfield slid down my rope. Zamora's rope wouldn't of held our weight. We grabbed our hosses and lit out up the gorge, around a bend of which Zamora was jest disappearing.

He had a fast hoss and a long start, but I'd of overtook him within the first mile, only Cap'n Kidd kept trying to stop and fight Bearfield's hoss, which was about as big and mean as he was. After we'd run about five miles, and come out of the gorge onto a high plateau, I got far enough ahead of Bearfield so Cap'n Kidd forgot about his hoss, and then he settled down to business and run Zamora's hoss right off his laigs.

They was a steep slope on one side of us, and a five hundred foot drop on the other, and Zamora seen his hoss was winded, so he jumped off and started up the slope on foot. Me and Bearfield jumped off, too, and run after him. Each one of us got him by a laig as he was climbing up a ledge.

"Leggo my prisoner!" roared Bearfield.

"He's my meat," I snarled. "This makes me seven! I wins!"

"You lie!" bellered Bearfield, jerking Zamora away from me and hitting me over the head with him. This made me mad so I grabbed Zamora and throwed him in Bearfield's face. His spurs jabbed Bearfield in the belly, and my cousin give a maddened beller and fell on me fist and tush, and in the battle which follered we forgot all about Zamora till we heard a man scream. He'd snuck away and tried to mount Cap'n Kidd. We stopped fighting and looked around jest in time to see Cap'n Kidd kick him in the belly and knock him clean over the aidge of the cliff.

"Well," says Bearfield disgustedly, "that decides nothin', and our score is a draw."

"It was my hoss which done it," I said. "It ought a count for me."

"Over my corpse it will!" roared Bearfield. "But look here, it's nearly night. Le's git back to the camps before my follerers start cuttin' yore Kansans' throats. Whatever fight is to be fought to decide who owns the canyon, it's betwixt you and me, not them."

"All right," I said. "If my Kansas boys ain't already kilt all yore idjits, we'll fight this out somewhere where we got better light and more room. But I jest expect to find yore Illinoisans writhin' in their gore."

"Don't worry about them," he snarled. "They're wild as painters when they smells gore. I only hope they ain't kilt all yore Kansas mavericks."

SO WE PULLED FOR THE valley. When we got there it was dark, and as we rode outa the gorge, we seen fires going on the flat, and folks dancing around 'em, and fiddles was going at a great rate.

"What the hell is this?" bellered Bearfield, and then Old Man Richardson come up to us, overflowing with good spirits. "Glad to see you gents!" he says. "This is a great night! Jack warn't kilt, after all. Jest creased. We come out of that great fight whole and sound--"

"But what you doin'?" roared Bearfield. "What's my people doin' here?"

"Oh," says Old Man Richardson, "we got together after you gents left and agreed that the valley was big enough for both parties, so we decided to jine together into one settlement, and we're celebratin'. Them Illinois people is fine folks. They're as peace-lovin' as we are."

"Blood-thirsty painters!" I sneers to Cousin Bearfield.

"I ain't no bigger liar'n you air," he says, more in sorrer than in anger. "Come on. They ain't nothin' more we can do. We air swamped in a mess of pacifism. The race is degeneratin'. Le's head for Bear Creek. This atmosphere of brotherly love is more'n I can stand."

We set our hosses there a minnit and watched them pilgrims dance and listened to 'em singing. I squints across at Cousin Bearfield's face and doggoned if it don't look almost human in the firelight. He hauls out his plug of tobaccer and offers me first chaw. Then we headed yonderly, riding stirrup to stirrup.

33

Must of been ten miles before Cap'n Kidd retches over and bites Cousin Bearfield's hoss on the neck. Bearfield's hoss bites back, and by accident Cap'n Kidd kicks Cousin Bearfield on the ankle. He lets out a howl and thumps me over the head, and I hit him, and then we gits our arms around each other and roll in the bresh in a tangle.

We fit fer two hours, I reckon, and we'd been fighting yet if we hadn't scrambled under Cap'n Kidd's hoofs where he was feeding. He kicked Cousin Bearfield one way and me the other.

I got up after a while and went hunting my hat. The bresh crackled, and in the moonlight I could see Cousin Bearfield on his hands and knees. "Whar air ye, Cousin Breckinridge?" says he. "Air you all right?"

Well, mebbe my clothes was tore more'n his was and a lip split and a rib or two busted, but I could still see, which was more'n he could say with both his eyes swole that way. "Shore I'm all right," I says. "How air you, Cousin Bearfield?"

He let out a groan and tried to git up. He made 'er on the second heave and stood there swaying. "Why, I'm fine," he says. "Plumb fine. I feel a whole lot better, Breck. I was afraid fer a minnit back there, whilst we was ridin' along, that that daggone brotherly love would turn out to be catchin'."

www.ingramcontent.com/pod-product-compliance
Lightning Source LLC
Chambersburg PA
CBHW030242180626
46810CB00008B/3250